PSSSSSST... **HEY, YOU!**

Are you afraid of
MONSTERS?

Do they make you
SHIVER and SHAKE
and shut your eyes
really tight at night?

If you think you're brave enough,
then come with me.

Come on.

Let's go to...

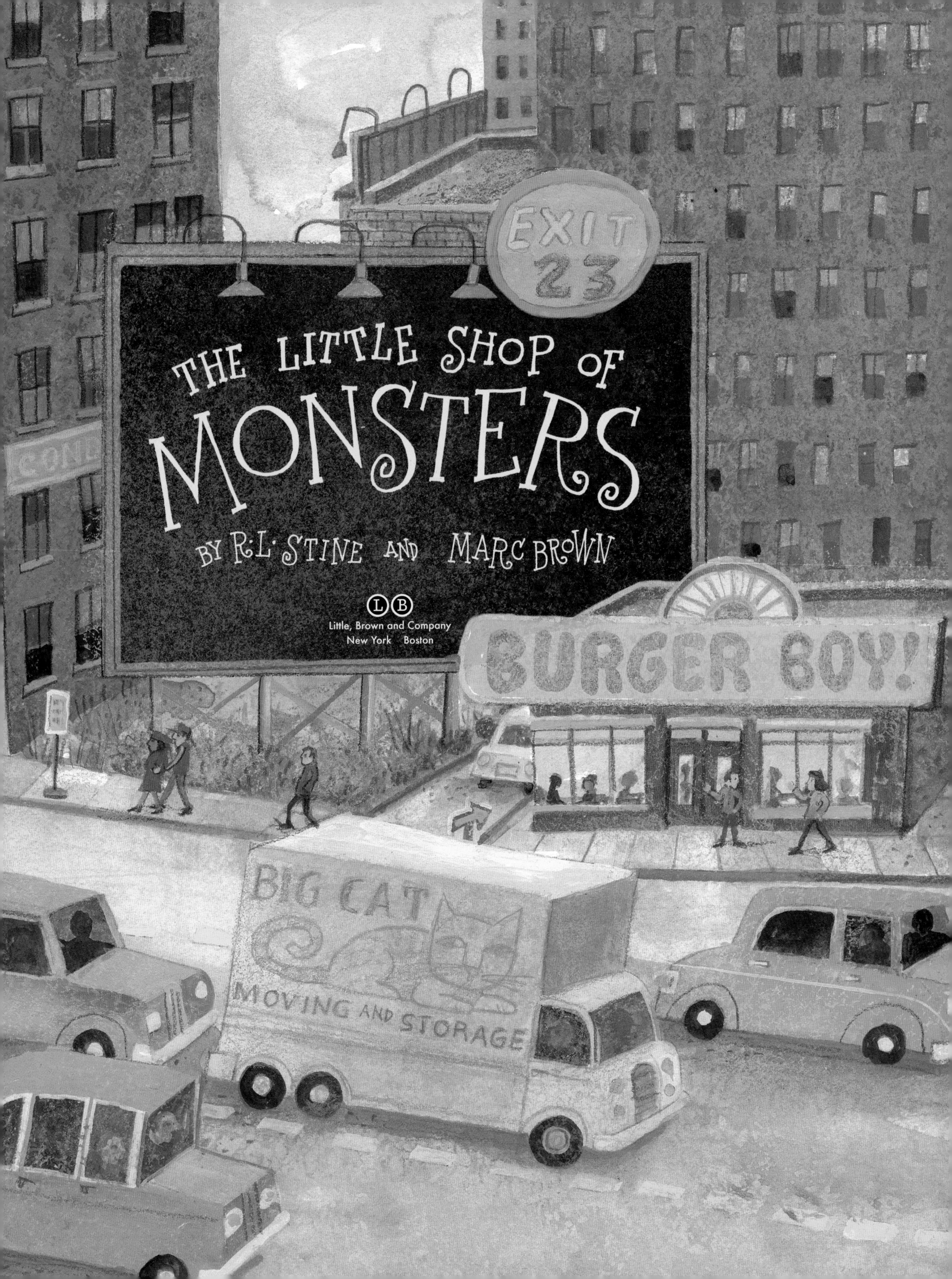

THE LITTLE SHOP OF MONSTERS

BY R·L·STINE AND MARC BROWN

LB
Little, Brown and Company
New York   Boston

EXIT 23

BURGER BOY!

BIG CAT
MOVING AND STORAGE

Here we are at the **LITTLE SHOP OF MONSTERS.**
Look at those big hairy monsters in the window.

I hope they don't **break** the glass, **jump** out, and **EAT** you.

(Would that spoil your day?)

This is the best shop to buy a monster.

I buy *all* my monsters here.

Isn't it cute how they **growl** and **snap** their teeth and try to **BITE** you when you walk in?

That's their way of saying hello.

(*Awwwww. So cute.*)

This monster's name is **SNACKER**. He loves to eat snacks all day long.

Go ahead. Say, "Hi, **Snacker**."
But don't shake hands with him.
Do you know his favorite snack food?

(That's right. Hands.)

Ooh, hold your nose! Hold your nose—and don't breathe! These are the **stinkiest, pukiest, rottenest, yuckiest** monsters in the store. Can you guess this monster's name?

(Hint: It rhymes with **PINKY**.)

And how about this guy? What's his name?

(Hint: It rhymes with **JELLY**.)

SNEEZER is a friendly monster.

She likes to snuggle close—and sneeze right in your face.

Look out! Here she goes!

AAAACCHHHOOOO!!!

AAACCHHOOOO!!!

I warned you.

You'd better get a towel and wipe the *sneeze* off this book.

(Yuck.)

This huge guy is named
BUBBLE-BELLY BILLY.
Look at that belly.

He eats everything he sees.

Do you know what's inside **Billy**'s big belly now?

I hope it's not your friend who lives across the street.

(That would be sad.)

These are **YUCKY** and **MUCKY**, the Yucky-Mucky Twins.

They're **ooey** and **gooey**.
They're **sticky** and **slimy**.
They're **goopy** and **wet**
and **clammy** and **drippy**.

Quick—stand back!
These twins love to **HUG!**

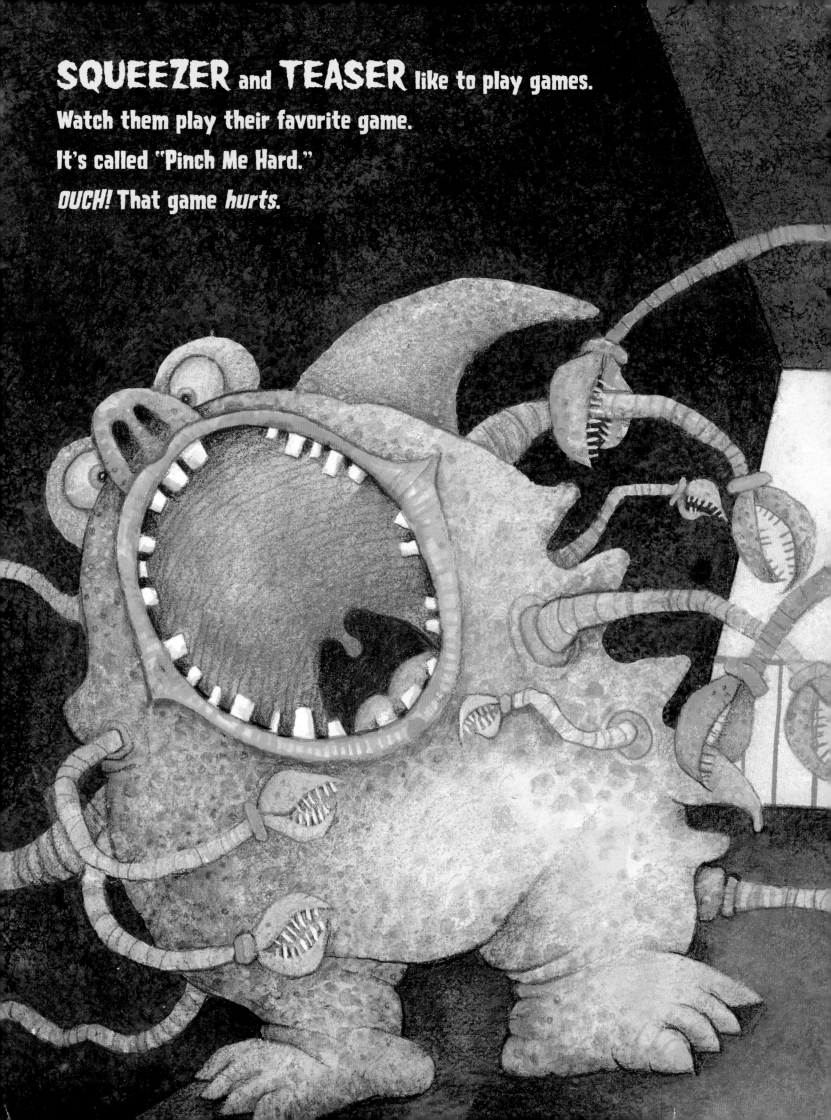

SQUEEZER and **TEASER** like to play games.
Watch them play their favorite game.
It's called "Pinch Me Hard."
OUCH! That game *hurts*.

But it's a great game for **monsters.**
(*WARNING: Do NOT try this at home!*)

Why is she called
TINA-NOT-TICKLISH?

Go ahead. Tickle her.
Tickle her again.
Tickle her a hundred times.

See? Nothing happened.
What did you expect?
She's **Tina-Not-Ticklish.**
(Are YOU ticklish?)

Shhh. Don't wake the **SLEEPER-PEEPER**.

This big hungry monster spends all his time sleeping under kids' beds.
Just think. Maybe there's *already* a hungry **Sleeper-Peeper**
under your bed, just waiting to jump out and scare you.

(*I hope I'm wrong.*)

You won't like the **PIGGLER-GIGGLERS**.

Look at them. *Hee hee hee.*
They giggle all day long. *Hee hee hee.*
They even giggle in their sleep! *Hee hee hee.*

What's so funny? *Hee hee hee.*
Uh-oh. Now here I go. *Hee hee hee hee hee hee.*
I can't stop giggling! *Hee hee hee hee hee hee hee hee.*
(I hope you don't catch it, too.)

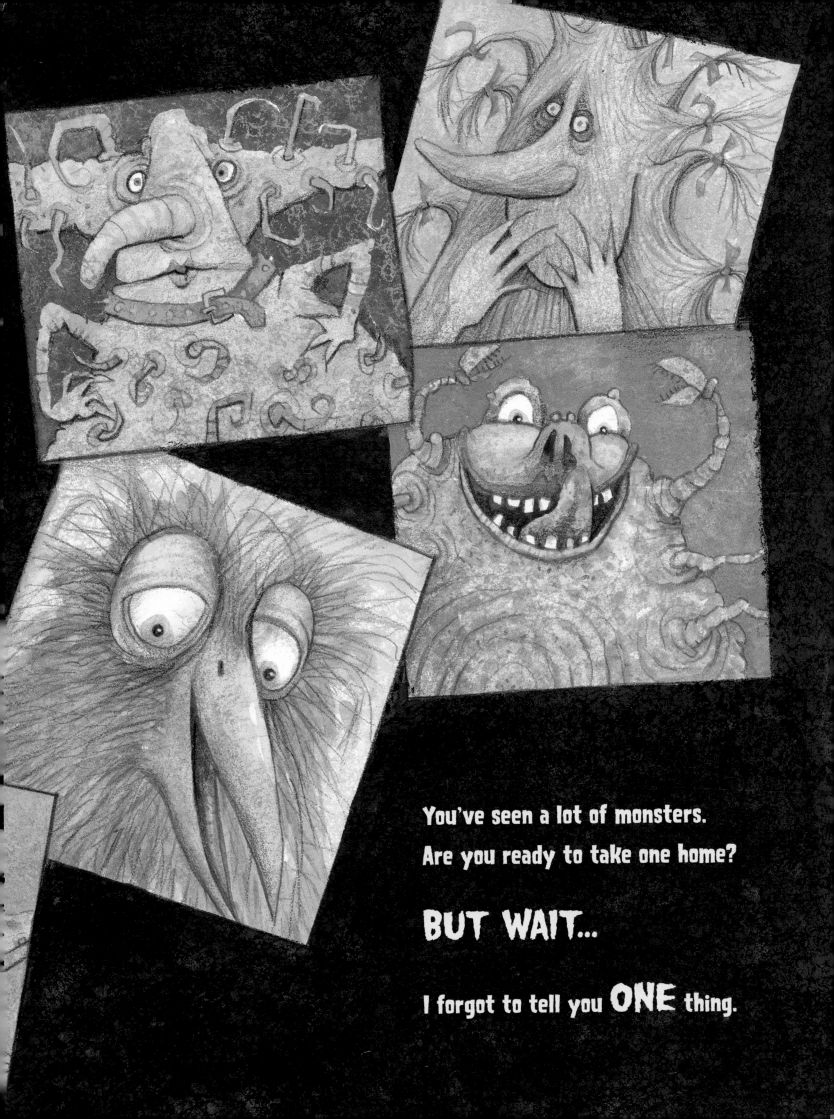

You've seen a lot of monsters.
Are you ready to take one home?

BUT WAIT...

I forgot to tell you **ONE** thing.

When you come to
the **Little Shop of Monsters,**

you don't **CHOOSE** a monster...

PHEW!

You just escaped!

Come back again soon.

Maybe *next* time you visit,
you'll find your monster.

OR...WILL IT FIND...
YOU?

FOR UNCLE SHELBY
—RLS

FOR IZZY, MY FAVORITE PET MONSTER
—MB

R.L. STINE is the creator of the Goosebumps series, which has sold over 400 million copies worldwide and inspired a popular television show and feature film, as well as the Fear Street series and many other spooky tales for children. He has also written dozens of joke books for kids. He lives with his family in New York City. His website is rlstine.com.

MARC BROWN is the creator of the bestselling Arthur Adventure book series and creative producer of the #1 children's PBS television series *Arthur*. He has also illustrated many other books for children, including *Marc Brown's Playtime Rhymes*, *If All the Animals Came Inside*, *Ten Tiny Toes*, and *Wild About Books*. Marc lives with his family in Tisbury, Martha's Vineyard. Marc's website is marcbrownstudios.com.

This book was edited by Liza Baker and Allison Moore and designed by Phil Caminiti with art direction by Patti Ann Harris. The production was supervised by Erika Schwartz, and the production editor was Wendy Dopkin. The illustrations for this book were created with colored pencils, watercolor, spray paint, and gouache. Various textural surfaces were used to build up many layers of color. The text was set in MonsterFonts, and the display type is hand-lettered.

Text copyright © 2015 by R.L. Stine · Illustrations copyright © 2015 by Marc Brown · Cover art © 2015 by Marc Brown · Cover design by Phil Caminiti · Cover © 2015 Hachette Book Group, Inc. · All rights reserved. In accordance with the U.S. Copyright Act of 1976, the scanning, uploading, and electronic sharing of any part of this book without the permission of the publisher is unlawful piracy and theft of the author's intellectual property. If you would like to use material from the book (other than for review purposes), prior written permission must be obtained by contacting the publisher at permissions@hbgusa.com. Thank you for your support of the author's rights. · Little, Brown and Company · Hachette Book Group · 1290 Avenue of the Americas, New York, NY 10104 · Visit us at lb-kids.com · Little, Brown and Company is a division of Hachette Book Group, Inc. The Little, Brown name and logo are trademarks of Hachette Book Group, Inc. · The publisher is not responsible for websites (or their content) that are not owned by the publisher. · First Edition: August 2015 · First International Edition: August 2015 · Library of Congress Cataloging-in-Publication Data · Stine, R. L. · The Little Shop of Monsters / by RL Stine; illustrated by Marc Brown. — First edition. · pages cm · Summary: An illustrated, interactive story with a narrator who invites the reader to meet a vast array of pet monsters, such as the Yucky Mucky twins, and choose one to take home. · ISBN 978-0-316-36983-1 (hc) — ISBN 978-0-316-34852-2 (int'l) · [1. Monsters—Fiction. 2. Pet shops—Fiction.] I. Brown, Marc Tolon, illustrator. II. Title. · PZ7.S86037Liw 2015 · [E]—dc23 · 2013046319 · 10 9 8 7 6 5 4 3 2 1 · APS · PRINTED IN CHINA